W9-AUQ-840

THE ADVENTURES OF TOM SAWYER

by MARK TWAIN

#5 Too Sick for School

Adapted by Catherine Nichols

Illustrated by Nonna Aleshina

STERLING

New York / London
www.sterlingpublishing.com/kids

STERLING and the distinctive Sterling logo are registered trademarks of
Sterling Publishing Co., Inc.

Library of Congress Cataloging-in-Publication Data Available

Lot #: 10 9 8 7 6 5 4 3 2 1
02/10
Published by Sterling Publishing Co., Inc.
387 Park Avenue South, New York, NY 10016
© 2010 by Sterling Publishing Co., Inc
Illustrations © 2010 by Nonna Aleshina
Distributed in Canada by Sterling Publishing
c/o Canadian Manda Group, 165 Dufferin Street
Toronto, Ontario, Canada M6K 3H6
Distributed in the United Kingdom by GMC Distribution Services
Castle Place, 166 High Street, Lewes, East Sussex, England BN7 1XU
Distributed in Australia by Capricorn Link (Australia) Pty. Ltd.
P.O. Box 704, Windsor, NSW 2756, Australia

Printed in China
All rights reserved.

Sterling ISBN 978-1-4027-6753-1

For information about custom editions, special sales, premium and
corporate purchases, please contact Sterling Special Sales
Department at 800-805-5489 or specialsales@sterlingpublishing.com.

Contents

A Big Test

Tom Sawyer was still in bed.

He did not want to go to school.

His class had a big test.

And Tom had forgotten to study.

Poor Tom!

Maybe he could study
before school started.
Tom jumped out of bed.
He opened his schoolbook.

Tom had to know all the state capitals.

The first state was Missouri.

Tom lived in Missouri.

What was its capital?

Tom couldn't remember.

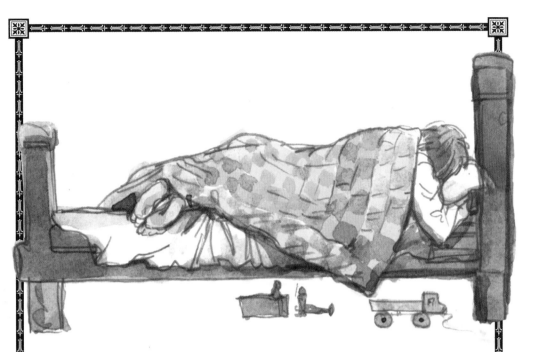

Tom dropped the book.
He climbed back into bed.
He pulled the covers
up to his neck.
If only he were sick!
Then he could stay home.

Maybe he was sick!

Tom touched his forehead.

It felt cool and dry.

He didn't have a fever.

He wiggled his fingers and toes.

Nothing hurt or was broken.

He looked in the mirror.

Was his throat red?

Tom looked some more.

Maybe his throat was a little red.

That was it!

He had a sore throat.

He was too sick for school!

No School for Tom

Tom moaned.

He listened for Aunt Polly.

She didn't come.

He moaned louder.

She still didn't come.

Tom moaned as loudly as he could.

Aunt Polly came running
into Tom's room.
"What is the matter?" she asked.
"And why aren't you dressed
for school?"

Tom moaned again.

Aunt Polly threw her hands up.

"Oh, my!" she said.

"Don't tell me you're sick!"

Aunt Polly felt Tom's forehead.

"You're not hot."

"It's my throat," Tom said.

"It hurts."

"Let me see," said his aunt.

Tom opened his mouth.

Aunt Polly looked and looked.

"Your throat looks fine," she said.

"Are you playing a trick?"

"No, Aunt Polly," said Tom.
"My throat hurts.
But don't worry,
I can still go to school."
Tom got out of bed
and fell to the floor
in a heap.

Aunt Polly gasped.

"Young man, get back into bed.

You are not going to school today.

Do you hear me?"

Aunt Polly tucked Tom
back into bed.
Tom tried not to smile.
Now he wouldn't have
to take the test!

Out of Luck

Aunt Polly brought Tom breakfast.

Tom was hungry.

But the only thing on the plate

was a piece of toast.

"Where are my ham and eggs?"

Tom asked.

"Rich food isn't good

for a sick boy," Aunt Polly said.

"Now eat up."

Tom pushed away the toast.

"Aren't you hungry?"

Aunt Polly asked.

Tom shook his head.

"You must really be sick,"

Aunt Polly said.

"Maybe fresh air will help," she said.

Aunt Polly opened the window.

"Look," she said.

"There's Doctor Robinson."

She waved at him.

"Doctor," she called.

"He's coming," she told Tom.

"Aren't you lucky!"

Tom sank lower into the covers.

He didn't feel lucky.

Not one tiny bit.

All Better

Aunt Polly went downstairs
to let in the doctor.
Tom made up his mind.
He jumped out of bed.
He put on his clothes
as fast as he could.

Doctor Robinson knocked
on Tom's door.
"Your aunt tells me
that you are sick," he said.
"What seems to be the matter?"

The doctor opened his bag.

Inside were many bottles of medicine.

Tom gulped.

The last time he was sick

the doctor gave him medicine.

It tasted awful.

He didn't want to take it ever again.

"I'm all better now,"

Tom told the doctor.

"And I'm late for school."

"I'd better have a look at you,"
Doctor Robinson said.
The doctor checked Tom's throat.
He listened to his heart.
"You are a healthy boy," he said.
"You may go to school."

"Thank you, Doctor," Tom said.
"I have to hurry now.
I have an important test."
Tom grabbed his books
and ran from the room.

At the bottom of the staircase,

Tom crashed into Aunt Polly.

"Where are you off to?" she asked.

"I thought you were sick."

"Doctor Robinson made me all better,"

Tom said.

"And I'll never be sick again.

I promise!"

Tom dashed out the door.
Class had only just started.
Tom shook his head.
As hard as it was to believe,
he was actually looking forward
to school!